LONDON, NEW YORK, MUNICH,
MELBOURNE, DELHI

DK LONDON
Senior Editor Ros Walford
DTP Designer David McDonald
Senior Production Controller Rachel Lloyd
Associate Publisher Nigel Duffield

Greenzys Llc – A production of Rethink Entertainment
and Media Inc. and MoonReef designs Llc
Editor and Art Director Lisa Keyser
Executive Editor Mark Lieber
Editor Adam Newman

Special Thanks
Elizabeth Daro, Stephan Keyser, Lee Rosenbaum, Sue Shakespeare

First American Edition, 2010.
Published in the United States in 2010 by
DK Publishing, Inc. 375 Hudson Street,
New York, New York 10014

10 11 12 13 14 15 16 9 8 7 6 5 4 3 2 1

Copyright © 2010 Greenzys Llc

All rights reserved under International and Pan-American Copyright
Conventions. No part of this publication may be reproduced, stored in a
retrieval system, or transmitted in any form or by any means, electronic,
mechanical, photocopying, recording or otherwise, without the prior
written permission of the copyright owner.

A Cataloging-in-Publication record for this book is
available from the Library of Congress.

ISBN 978-0-7566-6911-9

Mixed Sources
Product group from well-managed
forests, controlled sources and
recycled wood or fibre
www.fsc.org   Cert no. SA-COC-001592
©1996 Forest Stewardship Council

The papers used for the pages and the cover are FSC certified.
The inks used throughout are soy inks.

Dorling Kindersley is part of Pearson, a founder signatory
to the UN Global Compact. This sets out a series of
principles against which we measure ourselves in the areas
of human rights, labor standards, the environment,
and anti-corruption

Color reproduction by MDP Ltd, UK.
Printed and bound in the Unites States by Worzalla.

Discover more at
www.dk.com

Danielle Mentzer – *Writer*

Danielle is an acclaimed writer of children's books, family feature films, and children's television shows, including the worldwide hit series *Sitting Ducks* and the book *Plucked Duck*. Danielle's other writing and development credits include the Emmy Award-winning film *The Santa Claus Brothers*, *Pink Panther & Pals*, and *The Mouse And The Monster*.

Cris de Lara – *Illustrator*

Cris is an award-winning digital artist who has been recognized as one of the top 20 Digital Artists in the world by *PC World* magazine. She has also received awards as an artist and member of the Computer Graphic Society. Originally from Brazil, Cris currently teaches at Niagara College in Canada and contributes to its art website, which has been hailed as one of the top 5 websites on computer graphics, 2D, 3D, and animation.

A very long time ago, when the Earth was clean and pure, a young tree named Orinda sprouted up from the ground. For thousands of years, she stood strong and green, but then pollution began turning the rivers brown and the skies dark. Orinda became weaker and weaker. She was going to need a miracle to save her…

On top of a cold, rocky hill stands the oldest living thing on Earth—a pine tree named Orinda. Almost 5,000 years old, Orinda is very sick, but not because she's old. She's being poisoned by the polluted river flowing next to her.

Orinda remembers when the water ran clear and the Earth was pure and green, but the land is now dirty and filled with litter. At least Orinda will leave her pinecone behind after she's gone. It holds seeds that one day will grow into little pine trees.

One terrible day, disaster strikes! Grimy, a dirty, messy troublemaker steals Orinda's pinecone and races off. Her future sprouts are gone!

The ancient tree can only stand there, helpless. Tears begin to trickle down her bark.

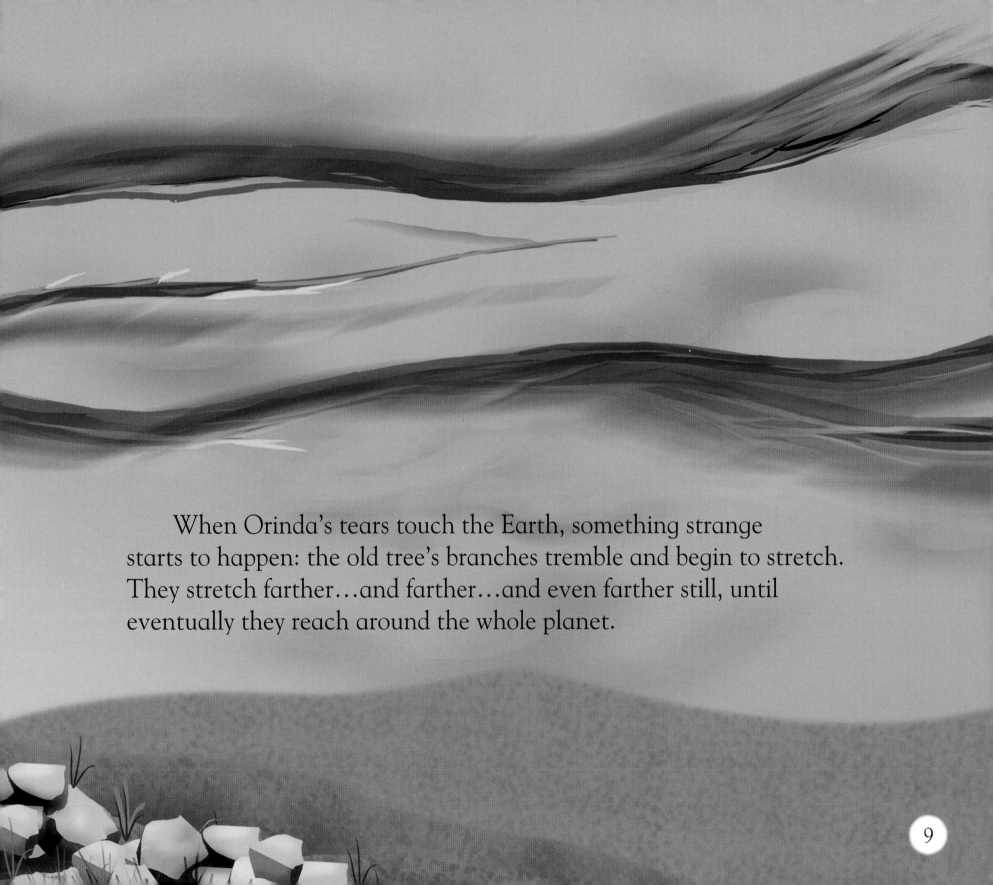

When Orinda's tears touch the Earth, something strange starts to happen: the old tree's branches tremble and begin to stretch. They stretch farther…and farther…and even farther still, until eventually they reach around the whole planet.

The first branch reaches a zoo in the United States where it finds a young giraffe named Violet. She is shy, but curious. The next branch comes upon a happy-go-lucky gorilla, Mango, in an African jungle.

Mango never pays attention to where he's going and he grabs Orinda's limb without even realizing it.

The third branch finds Poppy (a lioness) and her best friend Holly (a tiger) playing in a rescue shelter in Africa. They think the branch is a toy.

One of the branches stretches all the way to the top of the world, where it is tackled by Rooty the polar bear. Another stretches south to Antarctica, where it finds Peat the penguin leading a march.

A branch lands near Willow the elephant at a watering hole in India, who is amazed to see a traveling tree branch. The final branch discovers Yew Yew, a panda bear, in a bamboo forest in China. He is confused by this strange sight.

The branches magically bring the eight surprised animals back to Orinda. They stare up at her, wondering what's going on.

Orinda welcomes them and tells them about Grimy and her stolen pinecone. Then she asks if they will help to get her precious seeds back.

The animals aren't sure they can do this; Grimy sounds scary!
How can they catch him? Orinda gently touches each animal's
chest and a green heart appears.

"You will find your power here," she says, "in the love that you have
in your hearts. If you help me, you will also help the Earth."

The animals look at one another in amazement, but one by one
they agree to help. Then, something even more incredible happens…the
animals begin to turn green.

"This is so cool!" says Mango.

Peat shouts with glee, "We're Greenzys!"

The Greenzys hope that they can get the pinecone back to poor Orinda before it's too late, but they have no idea how to find Grimy. Violet notices a trail of slimy, black stains on the ground.

"Oil," she says in disgust.

Rooty roars, "This is our first clue. Let's follow the trail."

Willow tells Rooty that they can't just leave the oil. Now that they are Greenzys, they have to help the Earth. So, as they follow the oily trail, they scoop the oil into pails, which quickly fill up as the black puddles get bigger and bigger…and BIGGER.

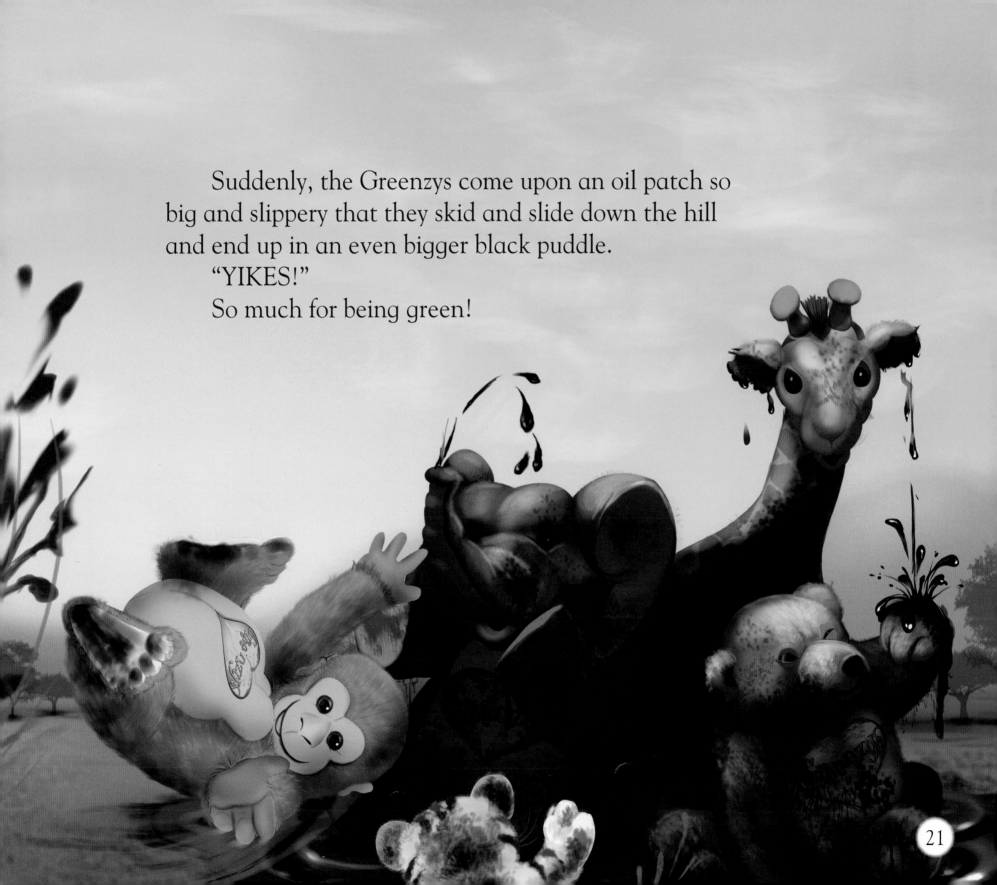

Suddenly, the Greenzys come upon an oil patch so big and slippery that they skid and slide down the hill and end up in an even bigger black puddle.

"YIKES!"

So much for being green!

21

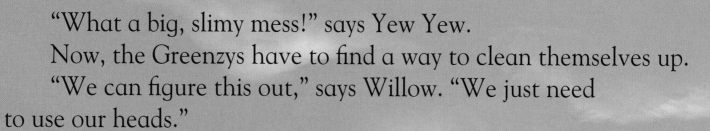

"What a big, slimy mess!" says Yew Yew.
Now, the Greenzys have to find a way to clean themselves up.
"We can figure this out," says Willow. "We just need to use our heads."

"Or your trunk," suggests Violet.

Willow takes the deepest breath she's ever taken and blows them all clean.

Then the team realizes there is a new problem: Willow has blown away the oily trail. Now what?

That's when they hear a ROAR that sounds like a jet airplane.

The Greenzys dash toward the loud noise and find a crazy, purple creature tearing up a beautiful grazing meadow with his scooter. They try to catch him, but he zips and zooms between them, then speeds away and disappears down the hill.

Having chased and cleaned up after Grimy, the Greenzys collapse on the ground, worn out and sad.

"How are we going to find Grimy now?" moans an exhausted Yew Yew. Mango looks sadly at the garbage floating down the stream and says, "Who could do such a thing?"

"Someone who doesn't care about fresh drinking water," suggests Violet.

Peat says, "There's only one someone like that."

26

"GRIMY!" yell the Greenzys.

If they go upstream to where the garbage is coming from they will be sure to find him—but will they be able to catch him?

"We have to stop Grimy to save Orinda," says Willow.

"And to save the Earth!" says Poppy.

Peat shouts "Go Greenzys, go!" and they're off and running again.

Upstream, the Greenzys come upon the dirtiest, most disgusting place they have ever seen. Empty soda cans, plastic bottles, and old scooter tires are piled everywhere. This trash could have been made into something new instead of ruining the land and water. What a green disaster!

Sitting smack in the middle of this foul place is Grimy.
He is using Orinda's pinecone as a backscratcher.

"There he is! And there's Orinda's pinecome!" shout
Holly and Poppy.

"Charge!" roars Rooty as he leads a mad dash for the pinecone. Grimy takes off running, but trips over a soda can and hits the ground—splat! The Greenzys land in a heap on top of Grimy and the pinecone goes flying over the dirty stream. They can't lose it now!

Willow reaches out as far as she can and catches the pinecone with her trunk. Whew!

It's time to teach Grimy how to recycle by turning garbage into things he can use again.

The Greenzys return the pinecone to Orinda. New, green pine needles begin to grow from her branches and the river beside her runs clear. She can smile again.

"The Earth and all its creatures suffer so much at the hands of careless beings like Grimy," says Orinda, and she thanks the Greenzys for their help.

The ancient tree asks the animals to plant her seeds in the ground beside her. Then she touches the ground and, suddenly, up sprouts a sapling.

The sapling will grow up strong and will be around for a long time…thanks to eight brave and loving animals called the Greenzys.

THE END

WILLOW

Willow the elephant comes from India and is
the leader of the Greenzys. She is always first
in line and blows her trunk like a trumpet.
Being a leader can be a tough job, but
to Willow it's worth the effort. She
loves the Earth and wants to
take care of it.

VIOLET

Violet, a giraffe, is the tallest and shyest member
of the group. She doesn't say much, but she
is very clever and knows everything about
how to be green. Violet's family come
from Africa but now she lives
happily in a zoo in the
United States.

Favorite Green Activity:
collecting rainwater and using her trunk
to spray water on her plants.

Favorite Green Activity:
teaching the other Greenzys
how to be kind to the Earth.

PEAT

Peat the penguin lives in the icy Antarctic near the South Pole. He cares about his home so he likes to clean up the litter he finds on the ice and in the ocean. He is always making useful, new things out of the trash that he finds.

Favorite Green Activity:
picking up litter, because it's bad for the Earth, for people, and for penguins.

YEW YEW

Yew Yew is a panda from China. He likes to relax and doesn't do very much. He spends his day eating bamboo leaves and sleeping, but he looks after the forest where he lives because without it he would have nothing to eat.

Favorite Green Activity:
growing bamboo because he loves to eat it. He doesn't eat anything else!

MANGO

Mango is a happy-go-lucky gorilla from Africa who loves playing and swinging through the trees. Sometimes he swings before he thinks and ends up in trouble. Mango is happiest when he is high up above the ground.

Favorite Green Activity:
helping the plants to grow by putting his old banana peels in the soil to rot.

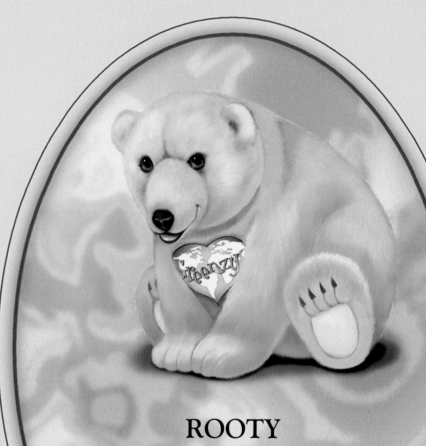

ROOTY

Rooty the polar bear lives in the Arctic near the North Pole where it is snowy and cold. He is grumpy that his icy home is melting because some people aren't looking after the Earth. Rooty can be tough, but he is very kind to the other Greenzys.

Favorite Green Activity:
making popsicles—they are made of ice and taste great.

HOLLY

Holly is a tiger who was born in the same
animal rescue shelter as her best friend
Poppy. She loves to joke around. Once,
she put a fake mouse in front of
Willow and made her jump in the
air. Holly is either in trouble or
looking for it!

Favorite Green Activity:
going on hikes—walking doesn't make the air dirty
and there are so many cool things to see.

POPPY

Poppy, a lioness, comes from an animal shelter
in Africa and is the youngest of the Greenzys.
She is also the most playful and she loves
chasing things. If it moves, she'll run
after it! Being green is easy for Poppy
because she always makes a
game of it.

Favorite Green Activity:
giving old toys to other cubs
so they can enjoy them too.

Greenzys Green Tips

💚 **Reduce, reuse, recycle.** Share a book or toys with your brother, sister, or friend. Reuse paper bags and newspapers—wrap a gift or make your own unique book covers! Ask your parents and teachers to recycle at home and in class.

💚 **Give to charity.** Ask your parents if you can donate toys, books, and clothes you don't want anymore. They'll get a new home and make another kid happy!

💚 **Don't litter.** Littering is bad news for your neighborhood and for the planet. Litter makes the streets dirty and pollutes our oceans.

💚 **Save water.** Turn off the water while you are brushing your teeth and tell your parents about leaky faucets. A dripping faucet can waste 20 gallons of water a day. Compete with your family for the fastest shower!

💚 **Walk or cycle.** Encourage your parents to let the family take walks or ride bikes together instead of taking the car. It means less pollution and is good exercise for everyone.

💚 **Turn off the lights.** Switch off the lights every time you leave the room. If you see an empty room in your house with the lights on, turn them off. You will save lots of energy.

💚 **Have fun without electricity.** Instead of watching television or playing computer games, play tag or hide-and-seek—or take your Greenzy for a walk!

💚 **Grow your own food.** Ask your parents to help start a garden to grow vegetables you can eat. If you don't have a garden, ask your teacher about starting one at your school.

SUPPLIED BY THE ENVIRONMENTAL MEDIA ASSOCIATION